MONSTER ISLAND

BEATRIX HOLLOW

FOREWORD

BLURB

Welcome to Monster Island Season 4, the deadly televised competition where felons, ex-military, and anyone crazy or desperate enough is dropped on an island of monsters. Winner takes all *if* anyone can survive.

I'm a bad girl—a convicted armed bank robber. It isn't the pardon, fame, or riches I'm after though. It's the monsters themselves. I've got a mighty hunger.

However, I might get *more* than I can handle when a grumpy green giant sets his red eyes on me.

CONTENT NOTES:

Extreme size difference, belly bulge, green nut butter,

violence, gore, death game, death/murder, guns, sexually explicit content, unsafe sex, mention of breeding (no pregnancy occurs), rough and extreme sex, unrealistic/would undoubtedly kill someone in real life sex, morally gray characters, and piracy.

CHAPTER 1
SAMMIE

"Have fun dying!" The guy behind me screamed. The sound of the plane drowned his words as he began shoving us out the back. Wind slapped my face roughly as my stomach leapt into my throat. My arms were blown out to my sides as I free-fell.

I lost my goggles somewhere between here and there, but squinting through wind-whipped, tear-filled eyes showed the island approaching fast from below. My fingers frantically grabbed onto the parachute release and tugged. My body jerked up as the chute opened. I had a few seconds of floating tranquility before the top of tall palm trees were smacking the soles of my boots.

Roars came from below us—monsters waiting for their chance at an easy kill dropping from the sky. This was the most dangerous part of the game.

We all began plummeting to the ground, all twenty-one of us flailing through the island brush towards waiting monsters that wanted to eat us alive. My parachute got trapped in a palm tree and without much thought I disengaged, falling ten feet to the sandy dirt below and taking off as fast as I could. A second's hesitation here could mean a brutal, bloody death.

"Welcome to Monster Island!" Danny, another competitor, screamed in furious mania beside me as we ran. The others took off in different directions as they disengaged from their parachutes. The crashing sounds of wild, blood-thirsty beasts came from all around.

Danny's boots slammed into the ground and he panted heavily. He was a thickly muscled man that had honed himself more for explosive heavy lifting than extended bouts of intense cardio. That wasn't keeping his enthusiasm down though. He was ex-special forces and half-convinced he was immortal.

My lungs burned as I ran through the island's forest. Sharp, thin palm leaves scratched my arms and cheeks. The thick humid air was unfamiliar and made me feel immediately winded as I gulped in deep lungfuls, savoring the novel jungle scents. Sweat began to collect under my arms and on my forehead. I'd be a drenched mess within ten minutes at this rate.

I turned my head, glancing behind me to see how close the monster chasing us was. He was brown, with twisted horns and hooves that stomped into the earth in a staccato of quick steps punctuated with great bounding leaps. He was furred from his hips down.

It was a satyr and he was coming closer with his horizontal pupils aimed at Danny. He lifted a gruesome, blood-stained club and my eyes widened. I could have opened my mouth to warn the guy. I didn't. I watched as the club hit the side of his high and tight haircut, a dull thud resounding loud enough that my own skull hurt. Blood immediately pooled in Danny's eyes internally before his body dropped.

Guess he wasn't immortal after all. Goodbye, Danny. And goodbye to whoever it was I heard screaming in the distance at my four-o-clock. Two competitors downed right away. We'd only been shoved off the plane and parachuted down a minute ago and the show was already in full, glorious action.

Monster Island Season Four. My eyes caught on the hovering globe following me. One of the many cameras tracking this colosseum style entertainment for the millions watching at home.

The odds were that none of us would survive. No one had in the previous three seasons. That was just the name of the game though. We were all desperate enough to risk the odds. The majority of us were convicts, myself included. It was either come to this fucked up little island and play with monsters, or rot in prison the rest of our lives.

There were the winnings to help boost the desire to be part of this too. Money, fame, and bragging rights. Which was why it wasn't just convicts now running through the woods. A lot of ex-military came to Monster Island. It was the biggest thrill any fucked upped individual could plead for. Danny wasn't the first god-complex to be proven mortal. I could practically smell the blood from past seasons wafting from the ground of this place. It reeked of carnage.

The round drone camera darted above me and another one just like it followed beside me in the trees. They were live-streaming my desperate race for my life, expecting me to die shortly. The whole world would be tuned in to watch, unable to look away.

Some called it a sign that our society was collapsing. Everyone else told them to shut the fuck up.

My tongue darted over my lips as I heard the hooves behind me getting closer. He was done bludgeoning Danny and I was his main goal now. I looked over my shoulder to catch a glimpse of his thick, meaty, monstrous body. His club dripped blood as his muscles bunched and rippled with his powerful movements. I watched his caprine legs move back and forth.

Everyone had their reasons to be here. They had spurted them off to the cameras, telling the whole world about their desperation or narcissism.

I hadn't told the truth when asked though. I'd lied my ass off because they probably wouldn't have let a freak like me come here if they knew the real reason.

I was a convict who had been doing a life bit for a botched armed robbery that resulted in a few civilian deaths. A pardon was most definitely a good motivator. I was a bad girl, what could I say? It was easy for everyone to believe that was the reason I was here. The bank robber bad girl wanted a chance to be free again—how cute. Now let's watch her get gutted by a monster.

Money, fame, freedom. Been there, done that. I was ready to mark something new off the bucket list.

I was the only one who knew the real reason I was here. My sopping wet pussy pulsed between my legs as I ran from the fat monster cock bouncing in the breeze behind me.

Fuck me, I loved monsters. I wanted to fuck a monster. Talk about life goals and I might just be minutes away from accomplishing mine.

"Shit," I gasped in delight, laughing as I jumped over a downed tree. I cleared it easily but I was tired of running. My thighs burned, my skin was scratched raw from plants, and I was about to have wet arousal sliding down my thighs because I could hear the loud snorts of the beast behind me. I wanted him to fuck me into the earth—a frenzied ground 'n pound.

Now that I was finally here the executives of the show couldn't stop me from my goal. I was in monster territory aka my own little red light district of desires. No one came to the island except the contestants. It was a guaranteed death. Which meant it was time to finally snatch my heart's desire—a meaty monster cock.

I fumbled on purpose.

"Oh, no!" I said dramatically, falling to the ground. I went down on my hands and knees, thrusting my ass in the air and wiggling it around. I looked over my shoulder and bit my lip. The beast stopped behind me, a confused look on its butt ugly face. It made me feel all tingly with frightened arousal.

"Silly me, I seem to have fallen." The brute knew something odd was going on but couldn't figure out the offering I was serving up. Come on you big monster, wet pussy is on the platter so gobble up. I groaned thinking about it.

"Come on, big boy. *Wreck me,*" I insisted. He took a step back like he was scared of me. Then he turned around and ran off. "Wait!" I cried out. He couldn't just leave!

"Where the fuck are you going!" I yelled, jumping up and running after him. He saw me coming and looked concerned. He sped up, his hooves slamming into the ground like a startled racehorse. I'd never been more offended in my life.

"How fucking dare you!" I spat, seething. I stopped running and pressed my hand to my chest while I tried to figure out what went wrong. Was I not attractive to it? That couldn't be possible. Satyrs were known for their libido. I shook my head and gave a disbelieving chuckle. No, he just thought it was some trap. He was too wary.

What I needed was a big, dumb brute. Something that didn't question a messy pussy asking for total destruction when they saw it. The idea really riled me up.

CHAPTER 2
SAMMIE

I started towards the supply drop-off, pulling the compass from my neck to make sure I was headed in the right direction. Everyone who had survived the parachute down and initial carnage would be going there to get at the stash of weapons and supplies. All the way there I grumbled in irritation, cursing all satyrs that ever existed but especially the scared little shit who ran from me. I pouted, thinking about the long brown cock he had flopping down to his knees. The missed opportunity made me groan in a complaint and tug on my long brown braid.

Things stayed quiet as I got close to the beach. The metal crates were on the sandy shore, waves gently rolling into the side of them. Wasting no time, I took off in a run towards the supplies. Immediately others darted from the safety of the plant line, exposing themselves. We were all in the standard clothes they gave us. Black tanks, jungle camo pants, and black boots.

Three men were racing towards the supplies along with me, fierce looks of determination on their faces. They wanted the first pick of the litter. Plus, last season someone had decided they weren't big into sharing. When they had arrived first to the weapons they'd turned them on the other contestants and gunned anyone down that came close. There was always a brawl at the metal crates but that season was the first mass murder.

Two of the guys arrived at the same time and worked together to rip off the top. The third guy plowed in and started tearing into the two guys, fighting them ruthlessly to get at the boxes first.

Men always had to make things more complicated. They were too busy fighting one another to give me any mind as I leaned into the crate and reached out towards the sleek, black guns.

A hand slammed on my shoulder and I was ripped back before I could grab it.

"Motherfucker," I snarled as my ass hit the sandy ground. Guess I was part of the brawl now too. One guy was ex-military but the rest of us were felons with penitentiary years under the belt. The trained fighter didn't stand a chance. He held up his fists and got his center of gravity under control. We leapt at him like starving hyenas on crack, sensing the odd man out.

A rumbling roar perked my ears up and I stopped pummeling the military guy's face with my fist. What was that? It came again but louder. The trees of the island shook and animals began crying out in alarm as something massive came running right for us.

The military guy was groaning in pain beneath me. The other two guys ran towards the metal crate, ignoring each other as they loaded up with guns in a panic. Someone shoved a pistol in my hand. We were suddenly all allies as the terrifying roar deafened us with its approach.

"It's a fucking big one!" One of the guys snapped out. I

gulped but didn't move, stuck in place. A green giant burst through the trees and my mouth fell open. Human skulls were threaded on a rope he wore as a necklace.

"Ogre!" One of the guys wailed. Instead of fighting, they took off running in sheer terror. I was still straddling the passed-out guy, my mouth hanging open in awe as the ogre raced towards the two guys fleeing. The monster was smiling as he did it, delight spread across his face. He was ready to plunder and pillage as much as he could in the situation.

I'd never seen something so big. He was probably ten feet tall and must have clocked in at about the weight of a bull rhino. He was thick—a big, beefy, bear of an ogre. The ground shook in time to each of his long strides. Muscles and a little extra that made him all the bigger. His chest was wide, his pecs meaty and plump enough that I wanted to press my face right in the middle of them and suffocate. The only thing he wore besides the bone adornments was a leather loincloth.

His face was topped with a thick mane of red hair, shaved at the sides but still thick enough to have in a braid. Tusks jutted up from his mouth, curling up towards his cheeks. He had a sharp, straight bone through his septum that could possibly have been a human femur at some point.

The skulls on his necklaces jostled together, clanking around as he reached one of the guys, wrapping his hand around his middle and picking him clear off the ground.

The man screamed and began shooting his pistol wildly. I had to scramble underneath the passed-out guy to protect myself from stray bullets. I heard screams grow high-pitched with pain alongside the crunch of bones. Then nothing.

Something slammed into the beach next to me and I jumped, flinging myself backwards. The top half of the man was staining the beach red beside me.

"No, nope. Fuck that," I said, gripping my pistol in my hand and leaping up, ready to take off as I heard the remaining guy's screams suddenly cut off. A roar shook the island around me as I tried to gain speed on the sand. It kept giving away beneath my feet, slowing me down and making my legs burn with effort.

Heavy stomping came behind me, getting closer at an alarming rate. It sounded like an angry rhino barreling towards me. My heart throbbed in my chest, pumping madly in fear. I wasn't getting away. That was clear. The ogre was going to rip me in two and not in the way I wanted.

I jumped into the forest, leaving the unprotected beach behind for the cover of trees. Not that it was going to help me much. Getting out of this alive was slim to none but I had something to live for. I hadn't fucked a damn monster yet and this dumb ogre wasn't going to ruin my life goal.

A roar shook the earth beneath my feet. I shoved the pistol in my sports bra and began to scramble up a tall palm tree. The tree wiggled as I gripped the bark and shimmied up. It was thin, having grown as tall as it could to reach the sun. Definitely not the ideal tree to climb.

The rage-fueled ogre barreled into the tree. The trunk bent towards the ground without breaking then snapped back up violently. Suddenly, I was catapulted through the sky.

"Fuck!" I barked as I flew through the air a good thirty feet away, landing as soft as I could in a roll. I finished the roll up onto my feet and looked up at the ogre. He glared at me with deep red eyes. My hand dove in my bra and I tugged out the gun. The beast looked momentarily stunned, halting his step towards me as he stared at my chest in surprise.

I snorted. Hadn't he ever seen breasts before? Hell, maybe he hadn't. I lifted the gun and his eyes snapped to it. As I started to squeeze the trigger, the ogre's eyes shifted behind me and widened. I felt the hairs rise on the back of my neck and dropped flat to the ground, rolling just as a massive sharp appendage dug into the ground beside me.

My mouth dropped open and I looked up to see a spider with a woman's face attached to the front. I weighed whether I wanted to fuck her or not. She blinked eight black eyes at me and hissed, lifting another one of her eight legs to spear me with.

Okay, guess she was off the menu too. Why was it so difficult to find a monster to fuck? You'd think they'd be hard up for it.

I had to barrel roll away, again and again, my head spinning as the spider lady relentlessly slammed her hard, sharpened legs into the ground in her attempts to kill me. I didn't even have time to shoot my gun, just keep rolling.

Well, until I hit a tree. My body stopped its movement.

"Fuck," I sighed, looking over to see spider woman smiling, fangs dripping venom as she lifted her leg for the kill strike. A camera hovered nearby, its lens changing as it zoomed in on my bloody end. A roar caught the spider girl off guard. Her eyes widened as she looked over and saw the ogre.

She began to speak in a hissing language to him. She appeared to be apologizing or maybe pleading for her life. Apparently, mister ogre was king of the jungle. She tried to move back and run but the ogre chased after her. They went into the trees and I heard screams and the sounds of ripping and tearing.

"Right, time to go." I hopped off the ground and ran. A moment later the ogre was behind me. Fuck, he was still focused on me. I shoved my hand in my bra, looking for my gun but only felt nipples and not much else. Then I recalled it had been in my hands when I was rolling and wasn't in my hands anymore.

I scanned the ground for something useful to use. My last attempt at survival was pathetic. I grabbed a coconut off the ground because island dodgeball was the only chance I had left. I was not betting on myself. I turned and lobbed it at his head. To my utter amazement, it actually hit him right in the forehead.

I thrust my hand in the air and gave a wild cry of success. The ogre gave a grunt but just kept moving. Shit. I took off again, knowing full well this was the end. No monster fucking for me.

Thick fingers wrapped around my middle and then I was being lifted up, the air violently expelled from my lungs as my body was jerked up from the ground. Before I could get my bearings I was tossed over his shoulder. He moved fast, pushing deep into the island forestry. My body flopped up and down like a ragdoll against his hard-muscled shoulder, the breath knocked out of me again and again in time to his long strides.

CHAPTER 3
SAMMIE

Before I knew it we were somewhere else on the island and he was laying me gently on the ground.

My vision was swimming, my head rocking back and forth as if I was still being carried. I heard a splash of water and a throaty groan. My head jerked up and I saw the ogre had slipped into a hot spring that gurgled softly next to me.

Miles of green skin was on display. His head was leaned against the grassy bank, exposing his neck. A thick Adam's apple as big as my fist bobbed as he swallowed. One arm rested outside the pool, the other was doing mysterious things under the water in a region I was powerfully curious about.

I should run. He'd just ripped a man in half with his bare hands. He had used human skulls like beads for his homemade jewelry. Also, it appeared the cameras hadn't been able to keep up with us. There was none in sight.

The ogre groaned again and it hit me between the legs. There was no mistaking what this ogre was doing. He was pleasuring himself in the steamy pool while the blood of my fellow competitors slowly washed from his hands. Lazily he looked over at me with hooded eyes.

Even I wasn't dumb enough to try seducing an ogre. The problem was, it seemed this ogre was trying to seduce me. I wasn't just thinking that because of my monster-loving gaze. The beast lifted itself up from the water, sat his very fine, plump ass on the edge of the pool, and continued stroking himself for me to see.

"Holy fucking shit," I mumbled, digging my fingers into the sandy dirt underneath me. His cock wasn't proportional to his size... it was even bigger. His loincloth was now tucked under his girthy monster cock, hiding whatever other beastly-sized monstrosities he had below. He fisted himself in his hand and gave himself a few short strokes, working himself into an even harder state.

The veins were prominent and thick on the sides of his cock. There was no doubt in my mind that if I wrapped my hands around him, I'd feel his pulse in those veins. He grunted, lifted up his other hand, and waved me closer.

Well, if I was going to fuck a monster, might as well go with the biggest, meanest one I could find. Pretty sure that cock was going to kill me. At least I was going to die my own personal hero.

I probably couldn't get away anyway, I reasoned. He'd catch up to me easily, pluck me off the ground like it was nothing, and then do what he wanted with me.... Over and over.

I pushed up and stumbled towards him. Any second now I expected my dream to crumble. That the ogre would stand up roaring spittle in my face, outraged at my presence. Instead, he flopped his waving hand back down and gave his thick cock a tight squeeze at the base. Green cum dewed up from his slit.

I sped up. I was ready to be plundered.

The penis' size was more impressive up close. I stood at the side of the pool shuffling around anxiously, waiting for the ogre to say or do something. Actually, I wasn't sure ogres could talk. A dumb brute monster with a giant cock. What more could a woman ask for?

He looked over at me appraisingly, eyes sweeping across my body as his fist slid slowly up his shaft. I looked at his cock and then back at his face a few times, trying to relay my desires to touch, suck, and fuck every monstrous inch of him. Actually, it was better to measure him in feet because of the sheer size of him—inches would take too long.

"You like what you see, human?" He asked, surprising me. He saw my gawking and gave me a questionable look. "Can you talk?" He asked.

"Can *I* talk?" I asked, flabbergasted.

"It speaks," he said with a snort of humor. The attitude on this one was already off-putting except he was still taunting me with his languid strokes up his meaty, massive erection. Whatever. He didn't need a good personality as long as he had that monster cock I wanted.

"You are human, right?" He asked, his tongue rolling up one of his tusks as he leered at me with greedy eyes. "Fuck, you are," he groaned, squeezing his massive cock harder to stemmy the deluge of green pre-cum that tried to burst out in his sudden excitement.

"I'm human. You're an ogre, right? I didn't think you were smart enough to talk."

"Well, that's not offensive," he snorted.

"You didn't think I could talk!" I countered, eyeing his fist moving up the length of his massive cock.

"Animals usually don't," he taunted, dark red eyes glittering in amusement when I looked at him aghast.

"I'm not an animal."

"That's good because it's not an animal I want to fuck. It's a human," he said gruffly. I snapped my mouth shut, my anger fizzling out. I gave him a more thorough look. His ears were long and pointed with thick human bones stretching out the lobes. There was a scar running across his face from an inch above his eyebrow all the way down to his top lip. He had prominent brows and a strong nose. His lower lip and jaw stuck out, the tusks jutting upwards from his mouth.

If I was into humans, I'd find this ogre ugly. I was not into humans though. I was into monsters and he looked like one of the biggest, baddest ones that existed.

"You want to fuck a human?" I tried to confirm with nonchalance. I eyed his cock and licked my lips.

"I've got this life goal," he grunted and my eyes zipped to his red ones. They matched his hair. Hair that wasn't just on his head but dusted over most of his body.

"Your life goal is to fuck a human?" I asked.

"Yeah," he grunted, giving his cock a tight tug. "Vicious little creatures with plain skin. I always thought it sounded fun to catch one of you, make you fuck my ogre cock. Women don't come here often." Talk about luck. This ogre and I were going to get along just fine.

"Funny, my life goal is to fuck a monster," I said.

"Oh?" He raised an eyebrow, a little smile curling the edges of his big mouth. Why was this ogre so damn smart? Clearly, someone had made a mistake, or perhaps this was the Einstein of ogres.

"So...you have a human kink and I have a monster kink?" I asked. This was the most perfect situation I'd ever come across. In response he grunted in approval and reached over, wrapping his hand around my entire waist and picking me up. Guess he was done talking.

"Fuck!" I yelled, flailing around in a panic until he dropped me on his chest. His hand smoothed over my back, feeling the shape of my body with thickly calloused fingers. My cheek pressed into his chest as I panted in shock.

"Yeah, so how about we fuck, little human," he said. He let go of his cock and began grabbing at my clothes. He tried to pull off my shirt and pants, jerking me around a little as he failed to get it off. Clearly, he planned to ravish me but all he was doing was giving me whiplash.

"Okay, okay," I snapped, irritated.

"Why do you humans wear all this?" He asked in distaste. I sat up and tried to wriggle my clothes off.

"You could have waited to pick me up until after I got naked," I complained. He reached up, gripped my clothes in his hands, and tore through them like paper. Suddenly my entire body was exposed, my breasts naked between us, my cunt hot and wet against his beefy green body. I was shocked at how quick and easy he tore into the fabric to get at me.

He tossed the clothes on the shore and not a moment later the ogre was trying to spread my legs while studying what was there. A thick finger slid across my pussy, digging around until he found the entrance. He rolled and pressed against my clit, making me give a breathy gasp.

This was really happening. I was going to get fucked by a monster. Finally, my dreams were coming true. My eyes lifted to the ogre. His eyes held mine, a little smirk starting to curl up the side of his mouth. I gave short gasps as he slowed his finger's movements and swept it around. He noted the way my body tensed with certain movements and I held my breath when he rubbed the front near my clit.

He watched me closely as he teased me but a moment later he pulled away. He pushed me backwards until my back was flat on his chest and my pussy was right in his face. Big fingers wrapped around my calves and pulled until the ogre's face was smothered between my legs.

The press of his tusks indented into me where my legs met my body. Hot breath spilled over my pelvis as his lips pressed into my center. He groaned against me in delight.

"Shit," I rasped, disturbed but delighted at how easily he maneuvered me.

"I love the taste of humans," he grumbled between my legs. Coming from an ogre, those words sounded terrifying instead of arousing.

"What do you mean by that?" I squeaked. A hot, thick tongue pressed into my lower lips. He gave my labia a few rough licks, familiarizing himself with my pussy. "Oh...*fuck*," I mumbled, stretching out on his body. His tongue dug into the bottom and swiped up, parting me open as his warm, wet tongue powerfully brushed every part of my pussy.

I cried out, my back bowing when it dug into my clit. He gave a few more long licks then realized the specific place that was making me whimper.

He pulled me back slightly and looked closely, inspecting my unfamiliar anatomy. Two of his fingers came up and, with much more delicateness than I would have imagined, he spread me, looking for the special spot he knew was making me wetter.

He needed me as wet and loose as he could get if he hoped to fit himself inside me. I wasn't sure it would be possible though, even if he worked me over for days on end.

That was okay, his tongue, fingers and big green, strong body covered in scars would be enough to make me limp away with a smile.

"What's your name?" He asked, pressing the hood of my clit up. He grunted in success at finding what he was after.

"Why does that matter?" I moaned as his big plump lips latched on to me and he began to suck. I cried out, wrapping each of my hands around just one of his fingers. They were as thick as baseball bats and easy to hold on to while he roughly demanded my arousal.

He pulled back.

"Don't stop!" I gasped.

"Name, little one. I want to know it."

"Sammie," I said with an annoyed sigh. I hated small talk. "What's yours?" I asked lifelessly. I could honestly care less but if he wanted to trade names, I could trade names. Anything to get his big, monster mouth back where I wanted it.

"Thracker," he grunted, face leaning in close to its meal again. His tongue pushed inside me, so big it spread me out and went in deep, making me shiver. His tongue undulated as he sucked on my clit. Hot breaths spilled down my body, his nose hovering above my hips since he was so much bigger.

Thracker's large, deep eyes held mine as I squirmed against his body. He tugged me harder against his face, his tongue pressing deeper and dragging against my walls. I could feel his teeth on my pelvis and ass, my entire lower half nearly enclosed in his mouth. A throaty noise came from me as my hips jutted forward, trying to ride against him.

One large hand pressed against my lower stomach,

forcing me still as his tongue did its work inside me, mapping out the human pussy he wanted to make fit his massive cock. I bucked, my hips begging to move, but he held me still easily as he did what he wanted. When he sucked hard on my clit I cried out.

Thracker's tongue was everywhere. A large wet, warm muscle licking me dumb. It was like he was really eating me. He could easily bite down and take a chunk out of me. Instead, his tongue rolled over me like I was hard candy, sucking and tasting, his mouth watering for more.

Long, hard licks moved me towards release at an infuriatingly slow pace. The pleasure languidly built, one tiny step at a time until I was desperate.

"Fuck," I whined. "Please," I begged, looking him in his eyes and trying to make him understand he was torturing me.

"Please," I whimpered when his tongue swiped up my clit again. He huffed in amusement and winked at me. Surprise zipped through me. He knew what he was doing and was doing it on purpose—teasing me higher, making me wetter.

He had to take his time, didn't he? With our size difference, he could easily ruin the fun all too fast and he didn't want that. No, he wanted to fit that cock of his inside me and there would be no fast way to do that.

I flung my head back and writhed against his chest and belly as he slowly sucked and licked. An orgasm grew closer and closer, all the while he kept holding my body still, not letting me buck against his hot tongue. I felt his hard tusks scrape against my inner thighs.

"Oh," I gasped and then I was unraveling in an orgasm. His tongue ran up my entrance and he noticed me clenching and unclenching between my legs. He pulled back in intrigue and worked his finger just inside, feeling my insides grip his fingertip tightly. I whined, loving the pressure of his thick finger.

"You're too tight," he grunted and worked his finger in deeper. My back bowed as I bore down on him, groaning in pleasure as I reached between my legs and frantically rubbed my clit, keeping the orgasm alive as much as possible as he breached me with his green, calloused skin.

"You like having an ogre eat your cunt, human?" Thracker asked with a gruff voice.

"You talk too much," I moaned. He began to work his finger in and out. My hips bucked against his finger, wildly riding it as he used it to fuck me.

"I'll talk all I want," Thracker said. My orgasm finally teetered away and he pulled his finger from inside me and pushed his nose between my legs, smelling me. He groaned and gave another quick lick, making me shiver.

"You already admitted you need my fat monster cock." He broke off with a groan, excited by his own words. Then he wrapped his hands around my waist and lifted me upright before pushing me down, making me wiggle until I was sitting on his thighs, staring at the massive green, throbbing cock.

"Put your human mouth on it," he begged with a rough rasp, practically quivering in excitement.

"Yes sir, " I said in awe. I'd never wanted something so bad in my life. I wrapped both my hands around Thracker's fat ogre cock. My fingers couldn't touch no matter how hard I squeezed him. He grunted and leaned back on his elbows, watching me and waiting to see what the human would do with his presented, hard girth.

I took a moment to appreciate its size. It was a thing of wonder and awe. The sad part was I now knew it could never fit inside me. He'd rearrange my guts. Even the tip might split me in half. It was a shame but that didn't mean we couldn't have our fun.

I slid my hands up his length, feeling the prominent veins as I made my way to his head. A drizzle of bright green cum dewed up, looking nearly radioactive. I leaned forward, my body pressing into his cock as I settled my mouth on the end and suckled. He was salty and earthy, a little musky too—a hundred percent meaty, manly monster.

Thracker groaned as I sucked the head. I loved the smoother texture of his skin here. I moaned as I ran my tongue over his slit, begging for it to give me more cum.

He gave a gruff noise and I saw him watching with smoldering eyes. His tusks curled out of his slightly ajar mouth, his bone jewelry stood stark against his green color.

I wanted him to look even more pleased. I wanted to make this monster be in awe of what I could do for him. Thracker nodded at me, encouraging me on. My tongue slid around, swiping around the circumference. My mouth trailed down the length of him, licking, sucking, and kissing.

I imagined him exploding in my mouth, hot spurts of green shooting into my throat and trailing out of my mouth in long streams. I imagined it coating my chest, its bright color like paint, showing everyone what I'd done to a monster. That I had got on my knees and was fed his meaty cock. I moaned while I kept worshiping him with my mouth.

My hands gripped him and moved up and down, making up for the fact I couldn't fit him in my mouth. His eyes creased as he gave a grunt of pleasure. As I sucked the tip of his cock he reached down and pressed a finger inside me. Then one huge finger suddenly became two, stretching me out in hopes my cunt could take his cock.

My hands slid up and down his length, twisting and squeezing beneath the head that I kept sucking with increasing demand. His hips rocked up to meet my movements.

"That's it, human," he groaned before he broke off in a roar. I felt the beast begin to violently throb in my hands and opened my mouth wide on his slit.

Thracker shot half of his cum into my throat, hot and thick. He kept me hooked with two fingers between my legs as he pulled away from my mouth. The smell of musky monster man filled my nose as thick jets of cum painted my body from my breasts to my hips.

His hand up my body, spreading his release in a mess all over me. Then two cum soaked fingers slid back inside me, pushing his cum into my pussy in purposely thrusts.

Thracker set me on the ground beside the hot spring before he stood up. Water fell in streams down his skin.

The bright green cum spread over me felt like a statement—my monster fucker status a lewd display all over my flesh. I'd been used by a monster and everyone would know.

I felt like a badass.

"I have half a mind to breed you, human. Force you to carry my spawn."

"Impossible," I responded. He bent down in the water, eyeing my pussy up close.

"You want to see more?" I asked and his crimson eyes lifted to mine. I smiled and spread my legs further, opening myself up for him to see. I was hoping he felt inclined to wiggle his fat tongue between my legs another hundred times.

"You're too tight," he complained with furrowed eyebrows. He arched an eyebrow before sinking two fingers inside me.

"Mmm, that's nice," I said, lifting my hips to ride his fingers. Thracker started to push a third in and a startling realization came over me. He was still trying to stretch me out to take his enormous cock that in no way could fit inside me.

"Uh," I said while he tried to go knuckle deep with three huge fingers. "This is awkward but I think we've reached the limit of what's capable." He looked up at me in irritation and then used his other hand to lightly pinch my clit. I squealed and bucked my hips while he kept working his three fingers in.

"Be a good little human, Sammie. I will see you stretched wide on my cock."

"You'll split me in half," I snapped. He pinched my clit again then began rubbing my entrance around where his three fingers were buried, appreciating the stretch of me.

I groaned in both pleasure and dismay. Each one of his fingers was roughly the size of a small baseball bat and I was *filled*. He kept rubbing on my clit too and it felt divine. In no way was I inclined to stop him from using his big ogre fingers between my legs. I'd just have to make sure to put a stop to it before he tried to squeeze his wide cock between my legs.

Although, I liked that he wanted to force his cock in my tight hole. Liked that he knew he had to work me open as much as physically possible to take him.

He wanted me badly despite our size difference. That thought made me groan.

He stretched me around his fingers and rubbed my clit. I felt hot breath and looked up, seeing him leaning over me.

The three human skulls on his necklaces hung down and brushed against my stomach. His tongue slid up one of his tusks as he kept eye contact, then he bent down and roughly sucked my breast into his mouth.

"Shit," I breathed out, feeling his hot tongue over my whole breast. It was a tiny morsel in his big mouth. His tongue rolled over the entirety of it, brushing over my nipple. Some of his teeth gently scraped my skin, making me shudder. He spread my legs wider then started to work a fourth finger inside me.

"I don't think it's going to work," I panted as he rubbed my clit, coaxing me to be compliant. His mouth popped off my breast and went to the other, working my nipples into wet points as he ignored my argument. He rubbed my clit harder as he tried to wiggle all his fingers in. I felt him push all four inside me and I grabbed his huge head, my fingers digging into his red hair.

Four ogre fingers were buried knuckle deep in my cunt, stretching me as he dug his thumb into my clit, making me feel pleasure despite the burn and stretch. I couldn't think of a time I'd been happier. Well, maybe that time I robbed the bank and thought I got away with it. No, actually this was better.

I cried out, my hips rocking back and forth, trying to race towards an orgasm I felt approaching. He slapped one of my breasts, watching it bounce and shiver. Thracker groaned in pleasure and did it again to the other breast. A pleasurable sting of sensation settled over my chest and I clenched down on his fingers.

The mounting pleasure finally crested and I started to cry out in release. He stopped pumping his fingers and looked between my legs as my muscles clamped down on him.

"I'm going to leave this tight human cunt with a permanent stretch," he grunted out.

"You won't fit," I moaned, riding out my pleasure. When I finally stopped clamping his fingers and was a satisfied mess on the ground, he stepped back. I nodded, happy he finally got the memo that his cock could never fit.

The loincloth he had tucked under his cock was suddenly gone. He flung it to shore somewhere. I wasn't sure where it landed because my eyes couldn't be removed from what I was seeing.

He had two cocks.

Two. Cocks.

"Why though?" I asked aloud as he reached around his bigger, main cock for the smaller one underneath. Although small wasn't really a word I'd use to describe it. It had to be a girthy ten inches. He fisted it, aiming it directly towards me, and then stepped closer.

"You'll take this first," he said. His meaty fingers rubbed at the round bulge halfway down his shaft. My eyes widened on that part.

I sucked in a breath and wiggled further away. I was happy but also freaking out a little because I'd already accepted it wasn't possible. He reached out, grabbed one of my thighs, and dragged me back down towards his waiting cocks. COCKS! TWO!

"Ohmygod ohmygod," I said, letting him pull me down until his second cock's head teased my entrance. "It's happening. It's really happening," I said with a burst of laughter. All my dreams were being realized. His bigger cock slid over my clit as he began pushing his other cock into me. I felt my body parting and spreading. It was the biggest cock I'd ever fucked but he'd worked me well with his fingers.

It slid in halfway and then I felt lots of pressure. I looked down and saw the bulge. It was a big round knot that kept him from gliding in more. His fingers touched where our bodies met, feeling how tight I hugged him.

"There's no way," I said. He looked up at me and snorted before he grabbed my forearms in each of his hands, holding them at my sides.

"You'll take what I have, human." He rocked out and then shunted back in to his bulge. I felt my body accept him to that point and it was more than enough. I moaned as he did it again and again, fucking me to his bulge over and over.

His tongue began licking at one of his tusks, his hooded eyes traveling up my cum coated body. My breasts swayed up and down as he rocked into me.

"Fuck!" I barked out as his bulge started to go in. He grunted, pulling out to do it again. He pulled on my arms, trying to work my body onto his bulge over and over. I felt myself stretching further open until finally the knot popped inside and I felt the burn of it.

He roared out as I groaned. I'd never felt like this in my life—this accomplished and used and full. His bigger cock slid up and down my body between my legs, sliding across my clit as he began fucking me quickly.

"So tight," he groaned as he rutted up in me, working me wide until the burn finally left and I felt only full and pleased. He tugged my arms and went balls deep, his body flush with mine. The bigger cock sat across my body, way past my belly button, showing just how massive and impossible it was. I tried to imagine taking it. Me a slobbering, drooling mess of contentment to fuck the biggest, meanest monster in every way possible. Thracker would roar in victory if he got it inside me.

I clamped my thighs tightly together so his bigger cock could fuck them. The ogre groaned in pleasure, nodding at me in approval.

"What a good little human," he growled. "My prize pussy for killing those human men." I liked getting his approval. I liked being called his prize. I liked making this big monster feel amazing with my body.

His bulge popped back in as he thrust and I moaned. All of a sudden he lifted me off the ground, holding me above the hot spring. I frantically grasped at his body before I realized he could easily hold me without my help.

Thracker began to use me like a fleshlight almost. He pulled my entire body up the length of him and then slammed me back down, giving a deep, long grunt. I felt his balls against my ass. The way he handled me like a toy made me feel all sorts of things, all of them positive. I'd never felt more wanted in my life.

He reached around and rubbed one of his fingers over my asshole. I clenched and tried to wiggle on his cock.

"I'm taking your ass, Sammie. I'm taking all of you," he said with a grough demanding tone. I moaned, the words causing me to shiver in delight. While deeply seated inside me, he reached between us and collected some cum off my body, getting it on the finger he clearly wanted in my ass.

"Shit," I said. He was strong, with thick slabs of muscle, but he also had a little gut. A big, beefy monster man. *My* big, beefy monster man. I wanted to fuck Thracker from now until the apocalypse. I wanted to be his human sleeve for the rest of my life.

His finger rubbed against my ass again, teasing the little hole. He pumped his hips a little and I felt his bulge rubbing inside me in the most pleasing way. I groaned, hovering over the water in his hold as his thick finger pushed in my ass, working it all the way in before he began pumping it in and out.

Before I knew it one finger became three and I was whimpering against him, reaching down to smear the cum from his bigger cock across my breasts like some sexual war paint. Who wouldn't be terrified of a woman who fucked an ogre?

"Thank you," I whimpered as he dragged in and out of me. I was living my dreams.

He suddenly pulled out.

"No!" I exclaimed in panic. I wasn't done yet! I wanted more. I wanted green ogre cum jettisoned up into my ovaries.

"Every hole is mine," he growled and I looked down and saw him lining up his smaller cock to go in my ass.

"Oh fuck!" I gasped. He pressed in. "*Oh fuck,*" I moaned. He grunted and grabbed me around the waist with both hands before pulling me up and down to his bulge the same as he did to my front. I knew what was coming. I was looking forward to it.

"Every part of you is tight, human. You'll be stretched too much for human men after this."

"Stretch me, Thracker," I panted and he grunted. I think I loved him. All I needed was a man with two dicks, a bulge, and who grunted when he used me like a flesh toy.

He began working me onto his bulge, twisting and grinding me against the fat knot. I groaned as it popped into my ass, burning pleasantly. My pussy felt needy and empty though.

"Such a good human slut," he groaned in delight as his bulge barrelled into me.

As he began to fuck my ass, my pussy clenched on nothing. I whimpered, both pleased he was buried in me but upset to have my front ignored. He looked at my face when I whimpered then he positioned his bigger cock at my pussy.

"You want my big ogre cock, human? Is that what you whine for?" He smirked and began working us together. Pressure blossomed between my legs.

"It's not going to fit!" I exclaimed, clawing at his chest as he tried to maneuver my pussy to take his way too massive ogre cock. He grunted in frustration and pulled me back slightly.

"I wish it could fit, Thracker, but there's just no way." I was disappointed in myself. I wanted it to go in. I wanted him seated inside me every way he could.

He carried me back to the shore, setting me down on my back. He pulled my labia apart, aimed his big cock at my pussy, and began grunting as he tried to thrust it in. I felt the pressure of it begging for entrance. I groaned in discomfort.

"It's not working," I hissed in agitation. He shot me a scathing look as if I'd challenged him. He reached up, gripped my shoulders, and began pushing me on his cock. I felt the head of his massive cock begin parting me as he pressed down on my shoulders and pressed forward with his hips.

"It's not going to work! I wish it would but it's not!" I exclaimed. More of his head slipped in and I glared at him. He glared back, a mean scowl made even meaner by his tusks. I reached out and grabbed his braid pulling on it roughly. He snarled in pain as I tugged him closer.

"It's not going to fit," I said slowly, trying to get across the point. I jabbed my finger in his chest. He growled like a freaking animal and then grabbed my hips and tried to work me on him. I began banging on his chest.

"You stupid ogre!" I called out and he grunted.

"Open up that tight human cunt for me to pillage," he growled in demand. I felt the burning stretch as the head of his monster cock popped into my entrance. He bellowed loudly, victorious. His entire body shook with intense pleasure to feel just that small part of me wrapped around his main cock.

I felt stretched beyond my limits but he was the one who needed to press his hands to the ground on either side of me and take a breather. That was how good I felt for him. It made the pain worth it, seeing the strongest, biggest beast on this island reduced to a full-body shiver and needing a break because of what I did to him.

His fingers rubbed at where my body was taking him with appreciation.

"You look so stretched and red. You couldn't be stretched any more than you are and you couldn't be gripping my ogre cock any harder." He broke off with a groan then grabbed my hips, pulling me further down on him. I felt his other cock slide between the cheeks of my ass as he pushed further in my pussy.

"Oh fuck," I groaned. Did I want this? Undoubtedly yes. Was It easy? No.

"Can you keep going?" Thracker asked, pausing. I'd never been more stuffed in my life. I felt like I was going to be permanently stretched for him alone. I couldn't imagine a human cock comparing ever again. A human cock was a miniature-sized toy not made for use compared to this.

"Yeah," I rasped out.

"That's a good little human," he managed to purr around his tusks. I felt a shiver of pleasure up my spine along with a tightening between my legs.

"Keep going," I begged. I felt the stretch, the burn, the

unbearable opening up that my body was doing to get the ogre inside me. He was so massive. I couldn't imagine a bigger cock existed in the world and I was taking it, being opened up and split in two so the ogre could fuck into my stretched cunt.

"Sammie," he groaned and I felt it in the base of my spine. Then suddenly he slammed my body down on his fat cock fully. I screamed, my body alive and throbbing with the massive fill of him.

He groaned, deep and raspy, then leaned forward and pushed his tongue in my mouth. It was too big for a real kiss. Instead, I felt like I was being fed his tongue as he thrust it deep into my mouth. I sucked on it and he groaned.

He tasted like bone and blood. My body burned like it was being torn in two as he pulled out and then began to push back in. He had to hold down my hips to make sure my body relented to the massive invasion he was making it take.

I whimpered and drooled as he kissed me, feeling as he pushed deep between my legs. He moved slowly and surely until I finally stopped whimpering and all I felt was full and stretched. The discomfort was still there, it always would be, but the discomfort felt like triumph and pleasure. It felt like an accomplishment and it kept me from forgetting what was thrust in my pussy—a giant ogre.

Thracker grabbed at his lower cock, rubbing the head at my asshole. He looked up at me, making sure it was okay with me.

"I want it all," I said in awe, feeling him pop in my ass—now seated in both my holes. I groaned, my head falling back. He slowly worked both cocks inside me, making me take more and more inches.

I couldn't take it all. I couldn't. I moaned as my legs were pushed as wide as they could go. I felt the bulge of his small cock pop in my ass and moaned gutturally.

"I'm going to breed you," he groaned, thrusting into me. "My human breeder." I looked down. Every time he thrust forward my belly bowed out, his cock forcing my body to bulge around him.

"That's right," I encouraged. "Use me, make me take it." He grunted and gripped my hips hard pulling me on him until I found it hard to breathe. He roared again and I felt it rumble through my entire body.

"I'll keep fucking you until you grow fat with my spawn. I'll force you to breed an army of ogres," he growled. I groaned and then the big ogre had had enough of gentle preparations, he was ready to fuck me senseless. He dragged out his cocks from inside me and then shoved himself back in roughly, grunting from the physical effort of his thrust.

I cried out, feeling so incredibly full. I felt crowded. I felt packed and he wanted to keep packing me, keep shoving more into the box despite it already being fuller than full. This was exactly what I had wanted. I wanted a monster to use me. To get off with my body. I wanted my body stretched beyond its limits to give a monster pleasure.

"Your tight human cunt and ass are the best thing I've ever felt," Thracker grunted.

I'd never felt so alive in my life. It was a high like nothing else. A hundred times more intense than the silly things I got up to before—the crime, the gunslinging, the bank robbing. I'd been a bad girl, wanting a life of intensity. I wanted to burn bright and die young. Today I was burning brighter than ever.

Mania came over me, making me laugh wildly, my

tongue hanging from my mouth as he grabbed my arms and lifted me from the ground. I was hoisted up, speared on both his cocks, and hanging in the air as he started to fucking destroy me. I was a babbling mess of pleased nonsense as I became his fuck toy—a sleeve for his two cocks.

I was stretched so wide around his monster cock that he was dragging across my clit with every brutal stroke.

He fucked like a fighter. He fucked like we were at war and he planned to kill my army. He growled and grunted, grabbing my hips to work me better up and down his shaft.

"Oh!" I cried out grabbing at his fingers, holding them like handlebars as an orgasm barrelled into me. It was a full-body experience and made even more extreme by just how stuffed I was. My ass sucked in his bulge cock, my pussy tightened around his bigger one, and I screamed as my heart beat hard in my chest. I looked down and saw the bulge of his cock appear each time he thrust inside me. It was a big mound in my body where he forced himself in to fuck me.

Thracker growled and slammed in harder as I orgasmed. I panted and whimpered then he ground me down on his cock, going deeper than he had been before. I gripped his forearms as I strained against the feel of him. His massive dick began throbbing hard against my stretched walls, pumping warm, thick, green cum inside my body until I was sure I could taste it.

He began to thrust again, roaring more. His roar was so loud it was deafening. It was brutal and mean and showed just how much he enjoyed my tight holes. Cum dripped and oozed from my pussy as more shot up inside me. Then I felt throbbing in my ass and his second cock began to spill his seed too.

I felt it warm and plentiful as it gushed into my ass. When he finally tugged me off of him, I was a mess—thick, green liquid all over me. I was sore, possibly internally fucked, and more satisfied than I ever imagined possible. He oh-so-gently laid me on the ground and I smiled in satisfaction.

CHAPTER 4
SAMMIE

Before I could fall asleep I realized one of the camera drones was hovering nearby. Several of them actually. There was even one close to the ground, aimed upwards for a different angle of the show we'd just put forth. They'd just live-streamed me raw dogging an ogre to millions of families across the world.

A static noise came from the drone as Thracker retrieved his loincloth and adjusted it back around his hips.

"Um, you've won," the show host's voice came over through the speaker, sounding unsure with his words.

"What?" I asked with a raspy, slurred voice.

"Uh... everyone else is dead and you aren't." The drone turned its camera towards the ogre then slowly shifted back to me. "If you can make it to the pickup area, you'll win."

"Oh," I said, the gears in my head slowly starting to move again. "Yeah, okay." I closed my eyes and got ready for a nap.

"You might want to hurry?" The show host asked instead of stating. Thracker came stomping over and punched the drone from the sky. It landed on the ground

36

and he stomped on it. When he lifted his foot it was practically flattened.

"You'll leave when I'm done with your human body," Thracker growled.

"I'll leave when I damn well want to," I shot back. An awkward silence came over us.

"You aren't leaving..." He stated in confusion, watching me stay nestled on the ground. Honestly, I wasn't sure I could get up if I wanted to. I *didn't* want to though.

"Not yet, maybe later."

"Later?" He asked.

"Yeah, I'm not leaving until I'm done with your ogre cocks," I responded, mimicking his words. Thracker's face spread slowly in a smile.

I was in no rush, what was the point of that? Apparently, I was now a free woman—a full pardon and half a million dollars. Which, in my opinion, could be a lot more. I'd had half a million dollars before. Hell, I'd had millions. Money had a funny way of being spent. Half a million would give me a few good times.

My tired gaze shifted around the island lagoon, taking in the impressive flora while basking in the intense humidity. A boat, I decided. I was going to buy a boat and I was going to use it to do a few heists, steal a lot of money, and be a very happy woman. Did that make me a pirate? I chuckled. Life was looking pretty good. I was currently rich and the most well fucked person in the history of humanity, my aching organs could attest to that.

"You don't have a cigarette, do you?" I asked, my voice a tired drawl as I stretched my arms and let my eyes slip closed.

"I have many things from the previous times humans have been dropped here." Thracker's voice grew more

37

distant as I visualized being on my boat. I was wearing the skimpiest little two-piece and compensated by having the largest hat impossible. I could hear the waves and feel the boat bobbing. The sound of gunfire was in the background, punctuating my team's ascent onto the cruise ship filled with a bunch of leisurely rich people just begging for someone to liberate their money and jewelry.

"Please take it, Sammie. We have way too much!" I imagined them saying.

A smile curved my face as I basked in the sun on my boat. There was a roar intermingled with the gunfire and I chuckled at myself. I guess I had it bad because here I was imagining my ogre in this future. A great green beast ripping people open like pinatas so that their gold would rain down into my waiting hands.

Something hard slapped my face and I bolted upright. I'd been sleeping and now I was somewhere dark and gray. Monster Island's showboat host was bug-eyed in front of me. He was svelte with brown skin and a tight one-piece made of spandex. Gold rings were on every finger and his hair was bright red and shaped in dramatic one-foot spikes.

He slapped me again, apparently because he simply wanted to—obviously, I was already fucking awake.

"Do it again and it's the last time you'll have use of that hand," I snapped. "Where am I? Where's Thracker?" The host pulled back his hand and ground his perfect white teeth, shaking his head as he stared in anger at me. He wanted to slap the shit out of me again, I could tell. He hissed and dropped his hand, probably realizing my threat wasn't empty considering I was a violent felon.

"I'm in deep shit because of you," he said, spinning around and lifting his arms dramatically. "You just *had* to fuck one of them didn't you?" He spun back around and got up in my face. "I knew there was something off about you the moment I saw your show intro."

"Oh please," I huffed, pushing him away and standing up to stretch my body. Oof, pussy, ass, and organs were still feeling like I fucked the horn of a rhino.

"I have a sixth sense for *bullshit*," he punctuated his words like each one was a bullet shot from a gun. His mouth pinched in anger.

"Where the fuck am I?" I asked again, stomping towards the door. When I grabbed at the door, the show's host reached out and slapped my hand like I was a kid reaching for a cookie before dinner was ready. I glared at him, giving him a further once over as my sluggish brain started to fire a little better.

His name was Lapis Lane. He'd been the show's tv host since its conception and people absolutely fucking loved his annoying, over-the-top personality. I'd even loved it until I woke up to him slapping the shit out of me.

"You're in the island's underground base," he said, cracking each one of his ring decorated fingers. I noticed the size of the rubies. "I sent a team to rescue you."

"Rescue me?" I asked, my words dripping with cynicism.

"Look we both know you willingly fucked that monster," he said, eyes rolling over my body in intense judgment.

"Okay," I shrugged, reaching for the door again. He slapped my hand. I gritted my teeth and stomped towards him. He gave a little squawk as I backed him up against the metal wall and slammed my hands beside his face, glaring up at him. He was freakishly tall, six foot six. I wasn't impressed.

"Get to your fucking point so I can leave," I demanded.

39

His eyes were bugging even more as he writhed against the wall, desperately avoiding touching any part of me. I could break this man in half.

"I fucking streamed it," he finally hissed. "Live!"

"Oh shit," I said with a chuckle. I moved away from him, rubbing my mouth as I delighted in the idea of every home tuned in to watch the first monster porn ever, starring my stretched pussy being pounded by Thracker's throbbing green cocks. I laughed, I couldn't help it.

"Ha ha ha," Lapis punctuated sarcastically. "The producers are furious. The public is in outcry and good ole Lapis is on the chopping block. I'll be ran out of the business unless I can fix this. And so, little miss porn star, we *rescued you*. Okay?"

"What?" I asked with humor. I wasn't understanding what was going on other than he massively fucked up and was angry at me for fucking an ogre.

"In my brilliance, I realized we just needed to move the plot along. Yes, we all saw you get fucked within an inch of your goddamned life. Yes, I did send the camera to watch. But we keep moving. We give the people something new to think and feel. Your rescue," he said, twisting to me and throwing his arm out as if introducing me to a crowd. I blinked at him and we stood there in silence a few moments before he rolled his eyes and dropped his hand.

"Clearly you were attacked by the ogre. Pillaged, ransacked, fucked. Your village was conquered!"

"Okay, I get it."

"And so the show shifted. Never before had the beasts been cruel enough to figuratively rip a person in half. It had all been literal up to that point!" I barked out a laugh. Maybe I still liked Lapis. Worse people had slapped me.

"I deemed that Monster Island was now Monster Island

Rescue. That the sweetheart of the show, the single winner in the history of our airing, had to be saved."

"Where the fuck is Thracker?" I asked. This was starting to bore me and make me angry. Them fucking up wasn't my problem. No rule stated we couldn't fuck the monsters.

"The ogre?" Lapis asked with a snort. "He killed two of my guys before the ten elephant tranqs finally took him down." Anger roiled up in me.

"I'm ready to go now," I said, grabbing the door and pulling it open. The metal hinges squealed as the heavy door swung inwards. I stomped into the hall with Lapis Lane hot on my heels.

"You can't go. You need to sign the NDA about what happened here."

"I'm not leaving the fucking island. I'm getting my ogre." His hand struck out like a snake and wrapped around my forearm in a vice grip as he came to a halt. I stopped and looked down at the hand. He quickly let go but still got in my face.

"You aren't going anywhere near that ogre again. Your monster fucking career is over. One and done," he said. "A one-hit wonder. You get it?" I leaned in closer to him and he leaned back, suddenly wanting space.

"I get it," I growled. Then I turned forward and kept stomping. Lapis quickly kept up with me.

"You aren't acting like you get it. Hello? Anyone home?" He asked, flicking my skull. I swatted at his hand. "The ogre thing is done. You're being shipped off the island and going on tour. My writers are already working on your script, your new personality, the emotional reactions you are required to display, how you wipe your ass, and every other aspect we think we can control."

"Let me think about it," I said. "Uh, no."

"Listen, bitch—" This time I twisted around, grabbed his shoulders, and flung him at the wall. He screeched, his thin body smacking the concrete and his eyes widening at me in disbelief and horror.

"Don't fucking call me that," I growled, slamming my boot into the wall right between his legs. He screamed and reached for his cock and balls.

"Noted," he wheezed. I dropped my foot and kept walking.

"But I'm serious. Your tryst with that ogre is done. Over, finito, wrapped up, sewn up, and tossed to the bottom of that fucking ocean out there." I stopped walking and stared at him, crossing my arms. He kept talking. "You aren't leaving this island until I'm sure you're going to play the best role of your life. You'll be rich, famous, and popular. You'll be the shining star of the show next to me. Hell, you can be the fucking co-host for next season's finale rewind. I'm offering you a spectacular opportunity so just fucking take it," he hissed.

"The problem with that, Lapis, is that I don't like people telling me what to do," I said without humor.

"Get over it," he snapped back.

"You do realize where you get your contestants, right? I'm not your average citizen and my dislike of being told what to do has sort of defined my fucking life. Hence the prison location you so graciously plucked me out of so I could star in your show for every gorehound across the globe."

He opened his mouth, ready to argue more. I cut him off.

"No, you don't get it. I really don't like being told what to do. It's a fucking diagnosable condition. You know what I did to get into prison for life?" I asked. His eyes darted around nervously and he cleared his throat, refusing to answer.

"I killed every man, woman, *and* child who told me what to do," I said.

"I know you did a shitty job of robbing a bank so you can stop with this bullshit. Remember, sixth sense for bullshit? But also, I'm the show's host. I know everything about you so please. I'm not scared of you," he scoffed.

I lunged at him and he screamed running down the hallway with me chasing him.

CHAPTER 5
THRACKER

When I awoke the island was dark, the trees shaking with monsters shifting in the night. My skull felt full of sand and water as I clambered to my knees. The waves of the nearby beach were a loud roar then a soft hiss as the water was dragged back out to sea. Bugs gave a low hum around me, highlighting how much my head throbbed in pain.

Something was wrong.

Quickly I climbed to my feet, swaying towards the dense jungle in front of me. My hands wrapped around palm trees as I tried to keep myself upright. The trees kept breaking when I put my weight on them, unable to support me. *Snap, snap, snap* between the heavy booms of my feet stomping into the earth beneath me.

The island shifted, listening to me for a moment, and then ran. The birds and mammals came alive in panic, rushing through the island's flora to escape the giant ogre. Only the bugs were dumb enough to stay close, buzzing in my ears and stabbing my skin to get fat on my blood.

I moved aimlessly toward the middle of the island, some unknown goal propelling me forward. Someone took something of mine. The realization made me grind my teeth as if my enemy's bones were already in my mouth.

It started to come back to me.

Stomp. There had been a team of humans in gear, different from the normal humans that showed up to be killed. *Stomp*. Gunfire. *Stomp*. Cold metal mosquitos shot into my arms and legs. I'd ripped them out and roared but felt weakened from their bite.

My anger was growing. My rage. The berserker inside me was starting to boil, a lava wanting out to destroy everything in its path.

Something was taken from me. Something important. Something I cared about.

A roar ripped from between my teeth, rage blasting the island. I could feel the earth shivering in fear beneath my feet as even the other monsters ran now.

Sammie.

They took my Sammie.

My hands wrapped around trees and I pulled. The muscles in my arms bulged, the veins throbbing as I ripped them up from the root and threw them.

An hour later I was regretting all the trees I'd pulled up. There was a line a mile long behind me and the berserker hangover was a vicious bitch. I groaned, flat on my back, staring at the dark sky and trying to count the stars to distract myself from the painful exhaustion soaked into my limbs.

A dark head popped into my view. Her long silky strands of hair hung down above me.

"Go away," I grumbled to the spider. She was always

annoying. A sneaky thing that watched with all her many eyes. She was down a limb, something I was responsible for. I didn't like her trying to kill my human earlier.

"I saw where they took her," she said and I whipped my head towards her. All those eyes would be useful today at least.

"Where?" I growled. She backed up quickly as I sat up, her seven legs twisting gracefully around themselves. Her eyes blinked at me. They were scattered across her human-like face, red and apathetic.

"The humans have a metal cave beneath the ground," she said, fangs protruding from her mouth. Humans were here? On our island? The spider saw my anger and dipped her head but kept her eyes on me.

"Yesss," she hissed. "They sneak around on our land. Unafraid of us while hiding behind their walls." I was angry again. I felt the berserker inside me chomping its teeth to come out again. Humans dared to walk on our land?

"Tell me where," I said. She smiled widely, her many eyes widening in delight. I lunged for her but her many legs made her fast. Long thin appendages moved frantically to help her climb a tree. Her heavy thorax produced a rope of web. Slowly she dropped from a branch, dangling down closer to me.

"Tell me where!"

"Promise me you will end them, ogre." *Demands.* I snorted.

"I would have ended them all already. They took what is mine." I looked up at the spider watching me. "And you will not threaten my human again when I bring her back." She blinked at me slowly, her many eyes watching, and didn't respond to my command.

"Behind the large waterfall," she finally said. I knew the place she mentioned.

"There is only rock there."

"The rock moves and behind it is their cave."

CHAPTER 6
THRACKER

I ran through the island. I could still envision the smile Sammie had shot me after saying she had no plan to leave. Perhaps I was a fool but I was okay to be a fool for her. To hope she never left.

Yes, I'd been fucked dumb. I'd never mated something that showed the indent of my cock as I shoved inside it. Any other human would have been terrified but she'd spread her legs and moaned as I forced her to stretch around me.

My cocks grew hard as I ran toward the humans. I reached down and shoved the loincloth beneath my first cock. My hand wrapped around the green length and I strangled it with my fist, trying to remind it of Sammie's tight cunt. I wanted to show the humans my manhood. I wanted their terror to be astounding as they saw the beast they'd wronged.

The waterfall came into view. I ran through and pounded on the rock wall. The berserker in me burst out, taking over. When I became like this, there was so much manic rage it blinded me. I needed that now. I wanted it.

These humans wouldn't simply be killed, they'd be destroyed.

The ferociousness increased my strength, making the veins on my biceps throb in time with the ones on my cock. My fist came down on the rock wall and went through the trick.

Fake rocks crumbled revealing I'd dented a metal wall. My fingers dug at the wall until I found something to hold on to, then I ripped it back. The sound of metal buckling and creaking was loud until finally the wall gave up and pulled free. I flung it behind me, not bothering to watch it fly through the sky and land somewhere miles away.

Men were running at me with weapons raised. Their metal darts couldn't stop me while I was berserk. I felt them pinch my skin but no poison could stop me now.

Reaching down, I gave my cock a sharp tug, making their eyes bulge in fear. I ripped the darts from my skin and roared, shaking the walls of their metal cave. The scent of fear wafted up from the men in front of me as I stomped forward, kicking one over before flattening my foot on his chest. I felt the floor beneath him and reached out for another, lifting him up and throwing him at the rest.

Blind manic rage took over after that. A blur of blood and screams, the delicious snap of human bones between my teeth, the beautiful explosion of skulls crushed between my palms.

A glorious battle for me. A massacre for them.

By the time I made it through their soldiers, I was still throbbing with unspent energy but only had corpses to fight against.

"Thracker!" Sammie called for me.

I stomped towards the sound of my delicious mate. I roared as I pushed through their small halls, ignoring the sensation of being trapped in a hole. The anxiety made me tentative but when I heard Sammie yell for me again I pushed it away and raced for her.

As soon as my eyes were on her the berserker in me settled.

She stood in the hallway with a large gun. One end rested on her hip and she was smiling at me, her eyes scanning my body from head to toe. I held myself taller, showing off the remnants of battle. If she were one of my kind she'd find this desirable. I feared our culture might clash here. Perhaps she'd turn away from me now, no longer attracted to the monster covered in the gore of her people.

"Someone let me out of here!" I heard someone yelling and banging. It was the same voice on the machines that flew around the island after the humans were dropped.

"I'll let you out once I'm done getting *reacquainted* with my ogre, Lapis. Seems he went through a lot of trouble to get to me," she said towards a closed door. Joy swelled in me. I shouldn't have doubted Sammie. She was not like other humans, she was a warrior. One who had a thick desire for all of me. My shoulders straightened and I flexed my body as her eyes scanned me all over, trailing across my chest until her heated gaze landed on my cock. Her eyes sparkled and she set her gun against the wall.

"Might take a while to get reacquainted with my ogre," she said, licking her lips and strutting forward on her boots. It was a shame she was wearing clothes again. I'd have to rip these to shreds as well. I wanted to see her mouth-watering flesh and the wet holes that called to me. Wanted to watch her squirm in my hands as I licked between her legs. Hold her in one hand as I slid her down the length of both cocks.

From the look on her face, she wanted much the same. My body was still covered in gore. Last time, I'd cleaned for her. Internally I warred with myself. I didn't like the idea of waiting but I didn't want to disrespect my human mate. After earlier, I'd decided to fuck her for the rest of our lives so it was best not to piss her off. Ogres were strongly monogamous once they found the partner they wanted and I'd found mine.

"I shall clean," I grunted. She snorted.

"Don't bother." She stopped right in front of me and reached out, wrapping two hands around the girth of my exposed cock. My head tipped back and I groaned as she slid her hands from the base up, twisting at the head before pushing her hands back down the length.

"Oh *no* you aren't!" I heard the trapped man say. "I am *not* staying locked up while you get your freaky on. Don't you know they are going to send a team? There are plans in place if monsters breach the underground!"

Sammie's hand didn't stop.

"He's probably lying," she rasped between plump lips. I wished she'd lean forward and press them to my tip, suck the cum right from the hole as her hands worked me over.

Alarms started to blare.

"I told you!" The voice yelled.

Punching through the wail of the alarm was the sound of machines. The thwop of the metal flying beasts in the sky, the growl of some large boat splashing in the water. An army was coming and it was likely to bring a force even greater than the one I just took out.

The berserker in me was tired, bringing out that rage and mania again would surely kill me. Regardless, there was no hesitation on what I would do. I twisted around to face the entrance and began to gather the rage beneath my skin. For Sammie, I would gladly die. It was a good death.

As I waited I heard nothing but the blood pumping in my ears. I held the berserker back, I had to time this right. I'd wait until the fight arrived and then unleash it for the last time. A smile spread over my face and I licked at my jutting tusks. This would be a great battle.

Sammie ran past me, a flamboyantly dressed man handcuffed to her wrist. He was wailing and tripping over himself to keep up with her. A gun was clutched in her other hand.

"What are you doing? Come on!" She barked.

CHAPTER 7
THRACKER

I moved behind Sammie, she and the human called Lapis were running as fast as they could. He kept screaming for help.

"Someone rescue me from this crazy person!" He yelled out. Despite his complaints, he didn't look too upset, just vaguely irritated. He kept shooting glares at me.

"You fucked her stupid and now I have to pay the price. If you two kill me I'm going to haunt your asses." I wasn't sure if Lapis knew how to shut up.

"Why can't we kill him?" I grunted.

"He's a hostage. They won't shoot at us if we've got him with us." Just then bullets kicked up the sandy jungle beneath our feet. They zipped through the trees, creating holes in leaves. Lapis began wailing high-pitched.

"Welp, guess they *will* shoot at him," Sammie laughed.

"Fuck y'all and fuck them too," he snapped. He began running with intention now instead of wildly flapping around. He even jumped out in front of Sammie and took the lead. "I am not getting shot today."

"Where the fuck are you headed?" Sammie asked him.

"My yacht. It's in a cove."

"You have a yacht on Monster Island?" Sammie asked, her words dripping with judgment.

"Well, not my yacht. Company yacht for the employees but I was the one who demanded it." More bullets came down.

"Consider this Lapis Lane's resignation!" He screamed towards the helicopter flying above us.

"Why does he talk like that?" I asked. Lapis Lane didn't talk like other humans. It was very dramatic, pronouncing some words with a flourish like he was performing for an invisible crowd.

I was barely jogging so that I could keep up with their slow pace. They were putting in a lot of effort, running hard. Humans were pathetic creatures. Though I'd keep that thought to myself to not offend Sammie.

"Talk like what?" Lapis snapped at me, glaring over his shoulder.

"Who cares how he talks. Lapis, take us to that fucking boat. I get the vibe I've just missed out on the rewards for winning the show so I'm going to have to take my prizes the old-fashioned way."

"Fine with me. These bastards are shooting at me like I'm not the whole reason the show succeeded!" He snapped loudly. They raced through the jungle, I kept a slow pace behind them, trying to muffle my loud steps so the helicopter wouldn't find us again.

Finally, Lapis ducked down behind some palm bushes, giving an irritated tug to his handcuffed wrist so Sammie would crouch down with him. I didn't like them being attached. I could easily remove his arm to solve that problem.

"Okay, down there," he said, pointing down the side of

the hill. From here it looked like it just sloped into the ocean.

"I don't see anything," Sammie said. I grunted in agreement.

"That's because it's hidden, dumbass," he snapped at her. I reached forward with a growl, wrapping my hand around him. He squealed like a bird. Sammie sighed.

"We need his help to get the yacht," she said.

"Do not call her names," I growled.

"Oh my god, you thought that was—" he cut off with a nervous laugh. "That's just how me and her talk. I see how you misunderstood." He forced more laughter out. "She loves it when I call her that. She calls me that too!" I removed my hand from him and his legs wobbled and he gripped his chest.

"Last I checked neither one of you knows how to drive a yacht!" He snapped indignantly. "We need to drop in the water and swim to the boat. There's a cave on the side of this mountain beside us. It's obvious from the water but hidden from the island."

"Okay," Sammie said. Lapis shot a quick glance at me.

"How about big boy stays behind to cover our backs." He licked his lips nervously. "Then when we pull the boat around he can get on." I was no *dumbass* but he was making it clear he thought I was one as well. He was trying to leave me behind. I kept my mouth shut and ground my teeth. He quickly filled in the silence with more chatter.

"We'll be sitting ducks. We'll hit the water and it'll be loud and then we have to swim and the helicopter is going to see us." He looked hopefully at Sammie.

"Okay," she agreed, eyeing the jump they needed to take to the water. Her agreement tore at me. She wanted to leave me behind as well. Perhaps I was just something to be marked off a list. Sammie had said that even—that it was a life goal to fuck a monster. Well, she had and now it was time for her to move on, leave the beast on the island and go be with humans again.

"Go then, quickly," I said, trying to hide how thick my words were. I'd protect her so she could get away. Then I watch her sail away. I'd been blinded by my own desires, not realizing how unrealistic my thoughts were. Of course, leaving the island is what she wanted and how could I fit into that? We were two different species from different worlds.

"You can handle them, right *big boy*?" Sammie asked with a smirk as she mimicked Lapis' nickname for me. I looked into her eyes, trying to search for something. I wasn't sure what. Could she tell how she was tearing me apart? I looked away. I didn't want her to know.

"Do not question an ogre's ability to fight," I commented gruffly. Sammie got up and reached on her tiptoes to grab my skull necklace. She tugged it and I bent over. Her mouth pressed to mine and I groaned against her soft lips.

"Thank you," I said as she pulled away. One last kiss was a good farewell present. She chuckled and slapped my arm.

"Alright let's do it!" She yelled then leapt off the cliff, dragging Lapis down with her. He began screaming and I snorted in annoyance before I roared loudly, shaking the trees to keep the helicopter from hearing them screaming and the splash when they hit the water.

Bullets shot around me. One grazed my arm. I liked the feel, the burn helped me forget about the way my chest ached. At least bullet wounds were a familiar pain.

I ran into the jungle. It went against my nature to watch

my mate leave. I was made to fight for her in every way, wasn't I?

My momentary restraint snapped. No, I wouldn't let her leave. She was mine.

I roared again and raced back to the edge of the cliff. I'd have to teach her she could never leave me. She said I was her ogre. Well, she was right.

I leapt off the edge and sailed towards the water. Swimming wasn't an ogre's forte. Too much dense muscle to have any buoyancy. However, I lived on an island and did my best. If the yacht was far away I'd just guaranteed myself a death sentence. It was impossible to stay above water for significant distances.

I hit the water and sank down, going deep into the sea. For a moment I floated in the depths, looking up at the surface and wondering if this was it. Maybe I couldn't even push myself back up to the air. I wasn't going to give up though. I needed to get to Sammie.

My arms pushed and my legs kicked. I let the berserker come to the surface for a moment and raged in the water, roaring as my muscles burned. I was expending energy I didn't really have, pushing my muscles past where they should go. My lungs hurt and my vision was red and black with rage and lack of oxygen.

But I kept on and on, not sure if I was even making progress. I'd endlessly swim until my death because I needed to get to my mate until Hades forced me to stop.

Suddenly, I broke water and let the rage go. I'd used everything and more to break the surface and now I could do nothing but gulp air before I started to sink again.

A net went around me and I was pulled up.

"Stop fucking around!" Sammie yelled at me. "We don't have time for dramatic drownings."

"Sammie!" I gasped. If I were a human I'd cry but I was an ogre so I buried all potential displays of weakness deep down inside. Luckily I could use my pent-up emotions to fuck her even harder when I got the chance.

"Yeah, yeah, big guy," she huffed, using a crank on the yacht to pull me closer. I gripped the edge and lifted myself up. She huffed and wouldn't look me in the eye.

"I know you didn't want me to come," I said. She glared up at me in offense.

"You don't need to be putting words in my mouth, okay?"

"You're angry I'm here," I said.

"I'm angry you nearly killed yourself!" She yelled, her face turning a deep shade of red. Then she began to hit my chest, beating on it with her fists. "Fuck you!" She yelled. "Making me feel things. Making me worried you'd died! Why didn't you wait until we were closer!"

Her puny hands did nothing but make me laugh. I grabbed her arms and held them.

"Don't laugh at me," she spat. My crazy bitch, Sammie.

"I was nervous is all. You're my mate."

"Don't go getting sappy now," she hissed, pulling her arms from me and stomping away. Even her ears were red. Ah, my Sammie did not like showing feelings either but I was not blind or a dumbass.

I noticed the broken chain of her handcuff and followed behind her. This boat was large and kept me afloat but I noticed that as I walked on the side the boat leaned in that direction, dipping towards the sea. However, we didn't go topple over so I ignored it.

"I'm going to need ogre-man to stay front and center while I try to steer us away from the helicopter aiming a rocket launcher at us," Lapis snapped, glaring at me as he gripped a wheel and twisted it. His jeweled hand pushed a lever and the speed kicked up. I fell over on the boat's deck and felt queasy.

"There's a good boy," Lapis said. "You just keep your green ass parked right there while—" He cut off screaming wildly and the yacht swerved. Something big hit the water. Sammie leapt forward and kicked a lever. The boat's speed increased even more as Lapis held the wheel.

An explosion went off behind us, water spraying up and raining down on us. The boat rocked violently.

"Fuck this," Sammie hissed and reached down, pulling out a very large weapon.

"Where in the hell did you get a rocket launcher?" Lapis asked.

"It's a yacht parked on Monster Island. The armory is the biggest I've seen," she said with a toothy smile, aiming up at the helicopter and shooting. The force of the weapon's blast shoved her backwards into the railing. The rocket launcher slipped from her hands and fell into the ocean.

"No!" She cried but a moment later a huge explosion came from overhead. The helicopter was a big cloud of smoke and fire, pieces raining down into the ocean as we sped away.

"Well that worked out well enough," she said, smiling at the both of us.

"Where to?" Lapis asked.

"Let's find a nice little island to lay low, then we're going to find a few cruise ships to pay visits to." I wasn't sure what all this meant and I was too nauseated to ask.

"Lapis Lane, pirate king! I like the sound of that," he said. He was a strange human.

"What do you say, Thracker? Gonna be my ogre on the

high seas?" She asked. My mate was going to make me spend the rest of my days sick. I nodded anyway.

"Fantastic. Let's go to that little resort island thirty sea miles to the west and I'll get a couple more crew members. Then we start pillaging some rich water villages. How does that sound, Thracker?" A large smile spread over my face.

"You sure you aren't part ogre?" I asked. Sammie laughed. I enjoyed the noise but my stomach squirmed and I started throwing up on the deck.

"You'll get your sea legs soon!" She promised with joy over the sound of my heaving.

CHAPTER 8
SAMMIE

Things couldn't be more perfect. I was sitting on the deck of my yacht and it only had seven bullet holes in it. I could hear the screams coming from the cruise ship above as I sunbathed in the skimpiest bathing suit I could find. It was practically two pieces of string more than a bathing suit. My hat wasn't quite as big as I'd envisioned but it was good enough. More than good enough because this was all a dream come true.

The deep, resonating roar of an ogre came from above. There was silence and then I heard shrill terror. Once a few of the people leapt off their cruise ship into the water I knew I couldn't waste any more time. My team got moody if I didn't at least climb the ladder and set my boots down on the lido deck, waved a gun around, flashed a smile for the crowd, and rallied everyone in to fill our bags with their jewelry and cash.

With a sigh, I lifted my mai tai and pulled the straw out. A moment later I'd gulped the remnants of the drink and was climbing the ladder up the side of the great white beast of a ship. Apparently, it was the largest non-military ship ever made. My burning thighs would certainly agree with that. The gun on my back shifted around on my greasy sunscreen-soaked skin. My almost perfect hat leapt from my head and was taken away by an ocean gust. I didn't bother watching it fly out to sea—this was a regular occurrence. I'd just buy a new hat, hopefully, one that was even bigger.

Finally, I got to the top and swung my feet over the edge. The sun hit my eyes, blinding me for a moment. Now I missed my hat. I shielded my eyes as I tugged my gun around. Blinking, the first thing I saw was him. Thracker was impossible to miss. He'd always be the first thing I saw —big, mean, ominous, green. My monster.

After playing fuck me eyes with his red glare and beefy green chest for a few minutes I finally gave the shivering crowd some attention. They were all ducked down, hands raised to shield their heads.

"It's her," I heard mumbled. The sound of my name, Monster Island, ogre, and some other details bubbled up. I smiled wide. I'd won the show and it had certainly made me rich and famous, even if not quite the way they intended.

"Alright people give us your money!" Lapis sang out, clapping between each word as he sauntered back and forth at the front of the deck. The people didn't move.

"Listen to Lapis or I'll tell my ogre to eat you!" I yelled over their racket. Everyone began scrambling and screaming as their shaky fingers pushed their goods at us. Thracker smiled at me. He didn't really eat people. I mean not civilians...usually.

Back on the yacht Thracker and I moved into the deluxe suit, dropping bags of gold by the door. I climbed on the bed, crawling in a way that made my ass sway.

Thracker was never late to a fuck. His hand grabbed my hips and flung me around. I landed on my back with a sigh, lifting my arms above my head and spreading my legs. He shifted his weight and the entire ship swayed. My bathing suit gave a sharp snap as he pulled it from my body.

There was a beam on the ceiling of this room, right where the bed was. Which meant I couldn't see Thrackers' face. He was so tall it marred my view from the neck up of him. He was an anonymous giant right now. A thick brute who'd destroyed my clothes and was now rubbing two thick fingers between my legs.

A groan rumbled from my throat and I writhed on the bed. My clit was being ground against by his exploring hand. My wetness coated the tips of his fingers and he growled, shoving his loincloth below his first dick and fisting it in his hands.

I sat up in bed and shifted to the edge, wrapping both hands around his massive girth. My lips settled on the head of his cock, tasting his excitement on my tongue as I felt the veins of his cock throbbing in my hands. I worked him over, twisting my hands around his length, enjoying the ridges of thick veins as I sucked on his tip.

"Sammie," he groaned, his words rumbling down into my bones. I was so wet I was drenching the blankets beneath me. From this angle, I could look up and see his red eyes looking down at me. Sometimes I caught him looking at me with softness, like now. To think I could break an ogre down to reveal such emotion was empowering and elating. I thought I probably looked at him that way too though.

"Fuck me," I rasped. Working always made me so horny. It was equal parts the thrill and seeing him standing above a wave of humans—comparing his size and strength and ferocity to common men. Fucking right after a job had become our ritual.

Thrackers' hand landed on my chest and shoved me roughly. My back bounced on the bed as I felt his cock slap the mound between my legs. He was gripping the base of his length and operating his cock like a club, pounding between my legs up and down before he pulled his hips back and lined up.

"Bare down," he growled, the only warning I got. My hands slammed onto the bed, grasping at the blankets and sheets with the hardest grip I could. His cock inched between my folds, one agonizing second at a time, peeling me apart. I could feel my pelvic bones shifting, spreading slightly. My teeth ground together and I groaned as he kept forcing his way into me.

This was the most thrilling part—when my body bucked and fought. I was burning up, sweating even. My thighs shook and my hips tried to thrash and wiggle away. Thracker grabbed hold of my middle, his fingers wrapping around my waist entirely as he held me in place.

He never paused while pushing into me. Never gave me a break. I loved this dazzling painful exhilaration as a beast took what he wanted from me, even if we didn't really fit. He'd *make* himself fit.

He did that now, pressing his hips forward and holding me as my body relented, finally giving up the fight. His head popped inside me and I gasped, the burn exquisite. Thracker roared and goosebumps popped over my skin. God I was sopping wet now, panting and shivering from making him roar just from breaching me. My pussy strangled the head of his cock and he shuddered.

Thracker pressed his thumb against my middle, beneath my rib cage, and then plunged into me quick and dirty. We watched as the outline of his cock barreled into me. The end of the bulge slammed into his thumb and Thracker rubbed it through my body, groaning and swirling his hips. I could barely breathe, the pressure on my lungs making me gasp for full breaths that barely came.

"What a tight fucking cunt," Thracker growled, pulling himself back out. I felt hollow, like a cored fruit. Then he slammed back in, hitting where his thumb held steady on my body. He rubbed his head again and I could feel him throbbing everywhere inside me. I was stretched so entirely around his cock that my clit was pressed against his shaft, rubbing against his green length as he pulled out and slammed back into me over and over.

My body was stretched beyond its normal means as I clenched around the cock in pleasure. My hands went to my belly and I rubbed up and down on the bulge.

"Good little human," he rasped. "You like being my cock sleeve, don't you?" I nodded. I could barely talk, out of breath as he moved into me deeper than ever before. God, he might kill me. I felt faint and my body ached but it was the best pleasure I'd ever had. He bucked into me and I groaned, my clit rubbing down the extra-long length and demanding ecstasy even as he fucked me like a toy.

The orgasm built through the extremes my body was being forced into. This was everything. It was nirvana. My eyes rolled into the back of my head as the giant beast growled and grunted between my legs, shuddering and thrusting as I strangled his cock with my body.

"Such a good human hole," he growled as my clit rubbed across his shaft. Despite the pain and stretch the pleasure won, breaking forth in an explosion. My entire body clenched around him as I started to come. He roared so loud I gasped and bucked, fight or flight kicking in even as I moaned and gushed on his cock. He shoved deep into me and throbbed. My entire body throbbed with it, feeling the hot gush of his cum explode inside me. He was as deep as ever and I could swear the taste of his cum was in the back of my throat.

Bliss settled over me, shaking me to my core until I was jerking in aftershocks. I'd never get this type of extreme fuck from anyone else. Hell, I didn't want to. Thracker pulled out and sticky green juice gushed from me, coating my thighs in thick monster cum.

Everyone knew who I was. Monster Island Season 4 champion. The felon that won the show by fucking an ogre. There wasn't a person alive who wasn't craning their neck for another taste of the salacious show Lapis had streamed live for them.

They claimed they were outraged at first. Sickened enough to fill their shoes with vomit. But when Monster Island got back on its feet and brought them season five there was an air of disappointment when no one presented their hole to a horny monster.

Every prime-time watcher was left clutching their remotes, deflated in their chairs. They were missing the shock and awe the show normally brought them. There was no coming back from watching someone railed within an inch of their life by a giant green ogre.

That was why the boat took a sharp turn as Thracker landed beside me on the bed, completely spent. He pulled my body on top of his and calloused fingers massaged my thighs.

"You make me see red," he grunted, eyes closed.

"Red?" I asked, drawing circles on his chest.

"I go berserk when I'm inside you, the only thing I can do is fuck you until your cunt has milked every wet drop from me. There is no other thought in my head." I chuckled, pressing a teasing kiss to the deep green nipple near my mouth. He grunted and gently smoothed his hand down my back. The boat kicked up speed.

"Ready to be a tv star?" I asked sarcastically. Monster Island Season Six was starting tonight. In a brash and insane twist the producers not only asked Lapis Lane—now rumored pirate—back on the show, but little old me and the ogre who'd taken me on live tv.

Everyone was outraged, screaming about the moral decay of the world, offended, sickened...but had their TVs set to record the show in record numbers. It was going to be the biggest season yet. People were salivating for a chance to be thrilled, disgusted, outraged, horny, and fucked up from the comfort of their homes.

"I was already a tv star," Thracker said. He didn't really care what we did. He followed my vision with a grunt, willing to tag along to the edge of the world without question. I loved my ogre, loved the love he had for me. Loved that even if I was his "crazy bitch" he went with it all.

Tonight was the night we went back to the place we met. There was a twist from all previous seasons. We were champions after all and Monster Island had proclaimed there can only be one champion. Which meant we were dropping down into the island with the rest of the fucked up contestants.

They wanted to take our champion title and they'd all die trying.

EPILOGUE

HANNAH

"Good the fuck luck!" The guy on the airplane wailed over the noise. Lightning flashed in the sky outside the helicopter's opening. Suddenly I felt the imprint of his boot on my ass as he none-too-politely punted me out of the flying vehicle. The asshole gave my rectum intimate knowledge about my underwear's texture.

A blurred watercolor of greens looked like a surrealist painting through my goggles. No amount of frustrated whipping made anything clearer. Over the rushing of air and pumping of blood, I could hear thunder growling in the sky.

With a hissed curse I blindly snatched up the parachute string and tugged. After a moment I heard the whirring of a floating camera and peeled my goggles off. Since I was going so slow they dropped, flying between my dangling boots and going down. I'd pulled the parachute trigger far before anyone else.

I sagged in the parachute while the flying, spherical camera tracked me. I could only imagine what Lapis Lane was saying and the howling laughter of people at home. They always made fun of the first person to deploy.

The other contestants were small beneath me, racing towards Monster Island until big red chutes bloomed up, looking like blood dropped into water. Soon enough they were all out of sight and I was still slowly traveling down.

As the camera kept a close eye, I sucked a smile back into my mouth instead of letting it blossom. I didn't deploy the parachute too soon because I couldn't see. I'd done it at the exact moment I wanted to.

The carnage below was already taking place. With any luck, my competitors would be torn to pulpy, red shreds by the time my boots landed on the sand. I wasn't going to rush in guns blazing like the dumbasses dying beneath me. I was going to play this game like the genius I was—avoid the initial carnage and relax as the bloated number of competitors was picked off from the drop-in.

My boots skimmed the tops of trees. It was time to slip away from the monsters waiting for us to fall and find a competitor to team up with. This was going to be so easy.

I planned to be a vicious two-faced bitch. Turn this game on its head and start playing mind games. They always picked the muscled idiots for the show but now I was here and I was going to change everything about how this game was played.

They'd never had someone like me on this show and that's because there was no one like me. I was equal parts cold-bolded and intelligent. Me talking to someone with an average IQ was like someone with an average IQ talking to a chipmunk. People were rodents in my opinion and I was a god in comparison.

Monster Island Season Six was my chance to show the world who I was. I could already hear the shocked awe of

Lapis Lane, stunned to silence for the first time in his life as I revealed the intricate mind games I'd play on everyone else. I envisioned the reverence on people's faces as they saw me in person. Men would drop to their knees to worship me. Women would kill themselves knowing they were nothing compared to me.

It was pathetic they were impressed by Sandra or whatever the fuck her name was. How hard was it to fuck a monster? I'd never bring myself so low. She was gross. I tried not to think about her too much. I barely ever thought about her really. She wasn't worth my time. I'd be doing the world a favor by unthroning her, revealing she was nothing special. Finally, people could stop embarrassing themselves by slobbering over her.

Okay, so maybe I thought of Sammie sometimes. Maybe I thought about her a lot. Maybe I had a shrine of her pictures with all the faces scratched out and couldn't wait to end her sad life.

My boots hit the ground—scratch that, they hit what was left of Sigmund. I'd fucked Sigmund. I'd fucked everyone I could in the bunker before our big day. I wanted to sow the seeds for potential teaming up during the game.

I steered myself so my boots would land right in the mortal wound on his belly. He wheezed. Guess he was still alive. I flashed the camera a shocked look and fluttered my eyes.

"Oh no," I said. My performance was Oscar-worthy. I stealthily lifted my foot and stomped hard enough that the wound ripped larger and he bled out fast enough to lose consciousness before dying.

"Whoopsies. What have I done!" I tried to wrestle a tear or two out but ended up turning my face towards the sky and letting the rain hit my face.

"Sigmund and me—" I choked out, looking at the floating globe camera. Then I shook my head as if I couldn't go on.

I turned away and rolled my eyes, hitting the button that made the parachute break away.

Nothing happened.

The ground shook. *Boom, boom.* The shaking and deep noise grew faster and closer. I tried to run but my chute was tangled with the trees and gave me minimal slack.

"Fuck!" I wailed. They gave us each a pocket knife to carry, it was the only quasi-weapon we started with. I pulled the knife from my cargo pocket with the intention of cutting the parachute off me. The rain slicked my hands and made me fumble the weapon. It dropped inside Sigmund's wound.

"You got to be fucking kidding me. You couldn't just leave me with the memory of a shitty fuck. Now you have to be a hole my weapon drops into. Thanks Siggy, you useless dead sack of shit," I ground out, kicking his side. He wheezed again.

"Christ, just die!" I kicked at him some more.

The ogre burst through the trees. *Shit.* I looked around. It wasn't supposed to go this way. I wasn't supposed to die as soon as I landed. I was too smart to die. I was supposed to get everyone left alive to kill the champions, then I'd stab them in the back and take the title myself.

"I'll fuck you," I blurted out to the ogre, grabbing at my clothes as quick as possible. He'd probably thank me for the fuck, no longer having to slum it with Sammie. I pulled my tank and sports bra down so my pale breasts flopped out. The great green beast loomed ten feet tall, his red eyes trained on my face.

"God, how stupid are you?" I hissed, scooping my tits

up in my hands and bouncing them around. I repeated my offer of sex in slower words.

"I don't think he's interested," another woman said. I looked over towards the sound. Lightning flashed, showing the current champion herself leaning against a tree. My lips peeled back from my teeth and I hurled myself at her.

Sammie made me so fucking angry. I fucking hated how everyone was obsessed with *her*. She didn't do anything to deserve it. She wasn't even that pretty and definitely wasn't smart.

Before I took two steps a giant green hand swatted my entire body. I felt all the bones in my body break before I went airborne. The chords holding me to the parachute snapped so I could keep flying.

Right before I died I heard Lapis Lane on the floating cameras around the island blasting the news that Sammie and Thracker were still the reigning champions and wow wasn't Sammie just so fucking cool and sexy and—

About the Author

Beatrix Hollow survives in a puddle of mud sometimes called East Texas. She writes morally questionable paranormal romance that frequently has horror themes. Sometimes there's even a strange kink and interesting appendage. She finds dark, steamy, and humorous themes fun.

Beatrix studied creative writing and psychology at Virginia Tech, used to be a professional ice cream maker, and enjoys looking at artwork of raccoons.

Also by the Author

Hookah Smoking Caterpillar

Monstrous, MMF Alice in Wonderland retelling. A very steamy fever dream.

Flawed Creatures

Ancient monsters in a modern setting. A MMMF polyam monster urban fantasy.

Run & Hide (Myths & Monsters 1)

Spooky why choose monster romance with ghosts and famous cryptids.

Cute but Psycho

Love and sex in a paranormal asylum for the criminally insane. MMMF polyam/why choose.

Blood and Secrets

MM vampire x vampire hunter story with obsession and pining.

Made in the USA
Middletown, DE
27 October 2023

41377721R00050